TOBY
HAS A DOG

AND OTHER BOOKS

Table of Contents

Toby Has a Dog

by May Justus

First published in 1949

© 2018 Jenny Phillips

www.thegoodandthebeautiful.com

Illustrations by Sanford Tousey

Toby Has a Dog

The Tollivers lived in a little log house in the middle of No-End Hollow.

There were three of the Tollivers. First, there was Father, who was tall and lean. Mother came next. She was short and fat. Then there was Toby who was about the right size for his age and going on nine.

There was also Molasses, a mule which belonged to Father. He had not been named for his nature, but for his coloring.

Missy, the cow, was a great pet of Mother's. "A gentle cow if there ever was one," Mother often said.

Toby had a hound pup, but the hound pup had no name.

"A boy should name his own dog." This was the opinion of Uncle Tobe on Yon-Side. Uncle Tobe had given the pup to Toby. "Name that dog yourself," he had said, and then he had added: "And be sure that you give him a suitable name!"

A suitable name! A name to suit a mirthful puppy, full of mischief.

One day Mother had caught him eating from a pot of beans which were cooling on the hearthstone. She had chased him out of the cabin.

"Greedy Good-for-Nothing," she took to calling him.

As for Father, he called the pup Rowdy Rascal. For the pup was always chasing Molasses around the barn lot, frightening a neighbor's team, or scaring the chickens off the roost.

But the hound pup paid no attention. He knew as well as anyone that he had no proper name.

"We ought to give him a suitable name before he is any older," said Toby.

"We might call him Worthless," Father said. "That would suit him to a T. All the other animals do their best to earn their board and keep. Molasses pulls the plow in the field—"

"Missy gives milk," added Mother.

"The hens lay eggs," Father went on. "The pigs grow fat for meat. But the hound pup? He's no good at all, no good whatsoever. He does nothing but make mischief. We might as well get rid of him."

"Oh!" cried Toby, and he drew a long breath. "We can't do that. We would hurt his feelings if he thought we didn't want him. And what could we do with him?"

"Take him back to Yon-Side where he came from," said Father. "If he doesn't mend his ways in a hip-and-hurry, that's what we'll do with him!"

This made Toby feel very sad. He hunted up the hound pup and took him off all by himself to have a little talk with him.

"Listen, hound pup," he said. "You've got to learn some manners. And we've got to think of things you can do to earn your board and keep."

"Woof, woof!" agreed the hound pup. He was always perfectly willing to follow Toby's wishes as far as he understood them.

Toby thought of several ways the hound pup could be helpful. He taught him to watch the garden

and keep out roving hens which liked to lead their
chicks there.

This pleased Mother. She began to say a kind word
to the puppy now and then.

Father had a fine turnip patch down in No-End
Hollow which the wild rabbits were rapidly ruining.
Father complained about them. If they kept on, soon
there would be no greens for the pot or turnips left
for winter.

"We'll see about that, won't we, hound pup?" said
Toby. Now and then he would take his dog hunting in
the turnip patch. This scared off the rabbits, and they
stopped going into the patch.

Father was tickled. He was very fond of turnip
greens in the summertime and turnips in the winter.
He stopped scolding about the hound pup and calling
him bad names. He even stopped talking of sending
him back to Yon-Side.

Toby was happy to know that his folks were liking
his dog much better. He said to himself, "Now
maybe they'll help me to think up a suitable name

for my pup."

But before this could happen, Old Man Trouble caught up with the hound pup again.

Sunday was Big Meeting Day on this side of Little Twin Mountain. Once a month the Circuit Rider came to preach in the little log schoolhouse to the folks on this side of the mountain. It was a great day. Then everybody came to hear a fine sermon, meet their friends, and eat a picnic dinner. The Tollivers always went to Big Meeting. They wouldn't have missed it for anything.

Toby thought happily about the good time that was coming. He loved to watch the big crowds, to hear the people sing, to sample so many kinds of food. If he

didn't understand the sermon, he could take a little
nap till somebody woke him by calling out, "Amen!"

On the Saturday before Big Meeting Sunday, Toby
helped his folks get ready. While Mother washed
the clothes, Toby kept the wash pot fire burning.
He went to the store with Father to help him bring
home some needed groceries. He chopped some
extra fine stovewood for Mother to use in cooking the
chicken, two different kinds of pie, and the pone of
gingerbread.

The hound pup tried to help a little too. He snooped
around the kitchen, ready and willing to clean up any
crumbs which fell on the floor.

"While Mother washed the clothes, Toby kept the wash pot fire burning."

This was how the trouble came about. It was a bad happening for certain. Mother was turning her pone of gingerbread out of the pan and dropped a few crumbs.

Wham—slam! The hound pup dived to get them and ran against Mother. The mischief was done. She dropped the gingerbread on the floor where it broke into dozens of little pieces.

The hound pup would have eaten these too, before Mother could stop him. But that very moment, Toby entered the kitchen room with a load of stovewood.

"Grab that pup!" yelled Mother.

Toby grabbed him with one hand and dropped his load of wood.

Smash—crash! The hound pup hardly knew what had happened. But one thing he understood—this was no place for him!

"Woof—woof!" he howled and made for the door.

Toby couldn't keep up with him. In his rush, the boy stumbled over the wood he had dropped.

Ker-splang-splang! Toby's heels went over his head as he tumbled clear out of the door in a somersault.

By this time, Father was on the scene. He had heard
the noise way out at the barn lot and had come as fast
as he could.

"Jumping jaybirds!" he hollered. "Whatever has
happened?"

"Look there!" wailed Mother. "Look at my
gingerbread on the floor—all broken to pieces. That's
what that greedy, good-for-nothing hound pup did.
Now I really wish he was back on Yon-Side where he
came from!"

"That rowdy, rascally hound pup! We ought to get
rid of him!" Father muttered, eyeing the gingerbread
on the kitchen floor.

"He meant no harm," Toby said, trying to say a good
word for his dog. The boy's voice was a little shaky. In
fact, he felt rather shaky all over after his somersault.

He looked around for the hound pup now, but the
little dog had quickly vanished. Toby guessed that
he had gone to his refuge under the porch. The dog
always hid there when a storm came up. He would stay
till it was over. Toby thought he had better let him stay

there awhile.

On Sunday morning, the Tollivers came out of their

cabin door dressed up for Big Meeting.

All three of them had on their Sunday clothes.

Mother was wearing her red calico and stiffly starched red sunbonnet.

Toby had on new overalls and a shirt that was nearly new. But what made him feel all dressed up was the

new rush hat with the bright red band. He had bought
it at Cross Roads Store.

Father was wearing his new blue wish-book britches
with shirt and necktie to match.

He was carrying the heavy picnic dinner basket
on his arm.

Toby's mouth watered when he thought of the good
things in that basket—fried chicken, biscuit bread,
apple and berry pies, jelly, jam, hard-boiled eggs, and
cucumber pickles.

"We've got the best dinner we've ever had for Big
Meeting!" Toby said, sniffing the good smells that
slipped from the basket cover.

"Oh," wailed Mother, "if only I hadn't lost my
gingerbread! I've always taken gingerbread for Big
Meeting dinner. The Circuit Rider likes it. He says it's
like the kind his mother used to make."

She gave a sigh as she followed Father down the
path in the yard.

Just then the hound pup crept out from under the
porch and ran over to Toby. Both of them dashed

ahead to the gate.

A frowning look darkened Father's face, and he spoke in a stern manner: "Reckon we'd better leave that rowdy rascal at home."

"Reckon we'd better," Mother agreed. "No telling

what'll happen if we take that good-for-nothing along."

"Woof, woof!" barked the hound pup, paying no attention to what was being said about him. He was eager now to hurry on to the happy adventures awaiting him. He never liked to stay at home when his folks were going somewhere.

On the few times they had left him at the cabin,

he had alarmed the neighborhood with his lonesome
barks and moans. Once he had nearly strangled
himself with the rope they had used to tie him up.
Another time they had kept him locked in the barn,
and he had wedged his head in a crack.

Toby was thinking of these things now. If they left

the pup at home, he would surely get into mischief.

The boy looked from Father to Mother. Then
he spoke up.

"Please, sir—please, ma'am," he said, "let the hound
pup go along. I'll look after him. I'll make him behave.
If he doesn't, I'll bring him home."

Father smoothed his new necktie and thought for a

long minute.

"All right, that's a bargain," he said. "You're to take the rowdy rascal home if he acts up, when he acts up."

"You're to take him home when he starts to act up," added Mother, "even if it's while the Circuit Rider's preaching, or in the middle of a song!"

"Yes, yes," Toby agreed. He was glad to give this promise.

He was very sure that he could make his pup behave and not have to bring him home. The dog could lie out in the meeting house yard till it was time for dinner, or

"Please, sir—please,
ma'am," he said,
"let the hound pup
go along."

crawl back under the floor of the meeting house.

"Woof, woof!" The hound pup dashed ahead in happy-hearted fashion, as if he knew that, thanks to Toby, he could go with the Tollivers.

Now Father, Mother, and Toby took the trail that led through No-End Hollow. The trail twisted and turned around the foot of Little Twin Mountain. A pleasant walk it was through a green and gold world of pine trees. The breath of the day was sweet.

Before they sighted the meeting house, they heard the sound of singing. Father started to walk faster.

"Reckon we'll be late," he said.

"Reckon so," Mother agreed.

"We're not very late," said Toby. "They're singing 'Praise God.' That's always the first song."

As they neared the meeting house, they could hear the song more plainly.

"Hurry!" said Father. "Let's get there before they end the song."

Outside the meeting house was a piney grove where people ate their picnic dinner. On the limbs of the trees many baskets were already hung.

Father looked to find a place where he could hang his own dinner basket, but couldn't find one in a hurry.

The first song was about to end.

Toby spoke up. "Father, you and Mother go ahead. I'll find a place for the basket, and then I'll come along."

"All right, all right," Father agreed. "That's a pretty good notion." He handed Toby the basket and started for the meeting house door.

Mother was close behind him. She called back over her shoulder: "Find that hound pup a place to stay. Then get him settled down before you come in!"

Toby had a notion to mind both Father and Mother.

He hunted around and soon found a strong limb to hang the dinner basket on.

Then he had another notion. He called the hound pup to the tree.

"Stay here," he said to him. "Stay here and watch. Do you hear, hound pup? Watch the dinner basket!"

Toby had taught the hound pup to watch for moles.

He was sure the dog would understand that he was to watch the basket. It was just as easy for the pup to see as the track of a mole run was.

The dog sat down under the pine tree. Then he looked up at the dinner basket hanging out of harm's way high above his head.

"Be good and behave yourself, hound pup," Toby reminded him, "and I will give you something good come dinner time."

"Woof!" barked the hound pup, as if agreeing to the notion.

Toby gave him a goodbye pat and hurried into the meeting house.

The preacher was starting his sermon, so Toby found a seat on the first bench he came to.

He saw Mother's bonnet way up front. Father was sitting in the Amen corner, and Uncle Tobe from Yon-Side was sitting beside him.

Toby would go up and speak to him after preaching was over.

Uncle Tobe always liked to have a little talk with

his nephew. He would want to hear about the hound

pup too. One thing he was very sure to ask Toby. He'd

want to know if the hound pup had been given a

suitable name.

Toby would have to tell the truth, though he was

ashamed to tell it.

Then Uncle Tobe would wonder why such a thing

had ever been neglected. To him it would look as if the

boy didn't care much for the dog that his uncle had

given him.

Toby was troubled over Uncle Tobe. He couldn't pay

any attention to what the preacher was saying. Besides,

if Father should ask him the text when they got home,

as he nearly always did, Toby wouldn't be able to tell

him. Yes, he was worried.

Then the Circuit Rider said, "Let us sing Hymn forty-eight— 'O Happy Day!'"

Toby stood up with the others. He liked this song, and he knew it by heart. But just as he started to sing, he heard a sound that made him stop. From the woods outside the meeting house came an excited, noisy, "Woof, woof."

The hound pup! He was raising a fuss, and this wouldn't do, thought Toby. Maybe he'd have to hurry off home with the pup.

Toby hurried out of the meeting house as quickly and quietly as he could. Then he gave a shout as he saw what was happening.

A thief had taken down the Tollivers' basket and

was making off with it along No-End Hollow Trail. Lickety-split went his long legs.

But the hound pup was at his heels! "Woof-woof!" he barked loudly. What a fine chase he was having! This was more fun than chasing Molasses around the barn lot or rabbits from the turnip patch.

Now Toby was racing too, faster and faster. Maybe he and the hound pup could get their dinner back.

"Boo—oo—oo!" yipped the hound pup.

This time the thief gave a shout and dropped the basket so that he could run faster.

Then Toby saw the wily face that gave one

backward glance.

"Traipsing Tom!" he cried aloud.

But the thief did not seem to hear the boy. Tom ran around a turn of the trail and went out of sight.

Traipsing Tom was a roguish, good-for-nothing fellow who, so far as anybody knew, had never done an honest day's work in his life. He spent his time going hither and yon all over Little Twin Mountain, stealing whatever he could from other folks. He had grabbed the Tollivers' basket because it was farthest from the meeting house door.

At least, that's how Toby figured it out. He and the hound pup sat down with the basket between them to get their breath.

The boy lifted the basket cover to see if things were all right inside it. And they were. All the food was there, but jumbled about.

"Everything's all hunky-dory, thanks to you, hound pup!" he told him.

All of a sudden, a notion had come *spang whang* into Toby's head.

"Whoop-ee! I've thought of a name for you, hound pup. It's Hunky-dory! Yes, sir-ee, a fine, suitable name!"

"Woof—woof!" the hound pup agreed happily.

As soon as they were rested, Toby and the dog started back to the meeting. Toby brought the heavy picnic basket to Mother and Father. He told them the whole story as they waited for him in the piney grove.

They liked the pup's name too. So did everyone else at the picnic feast.

"Hurrah for Hunky-dory, I say," Father added. "He saved our dinner for us. He deserves a treat."

And Father gave him a big piece of pie.

"Traipsing Tom was a roguish, good-for-nothing fellow."

"Bless his little heart," said Mother. "The next time I bake gingerbread, I'll save him a big slice to eat."

Uncle Tobe was very much pleased and fairly tickled to pieces over his namesake and his dog.

His eyes twinkled. "You're both all right," he said. "Your names are too. Seems to me as if you both had sure-enough suitable names!"

Lester and His Hound Pup

By May Justus

First published in 1960

© 2018 Jenny Phillips

www.thegoodandthebeautiful.com

Illustrations by Joan Balfour Payne

Lester and his pappy, Big Les, lived away up No-End Hollow where it curls around and between the mountains called Big Twin and Little Twin. They lived in a one-room cabin set in the middle of a yard which was always a noisy place, full of dogs. Big Les raised foxhounds, and Lester helped him.

They had started raising foxhounds for fun, to take fox hunting. This was the favorite sport of the mountain men and boys. And since Big Les had the finest dogs in the whole country, somebody was always trying to buy one from him. Sometimes they

offered cash, or, if they had no money, they would swap something they had in trade: a well-cured ham, a beehive full of honey, a can of molasses, or a bag of meal. Once in a while, Big Les would sell a dog on credit. That means the man would promise to pay the price soon. He knew that most of his neighbors were honest and would pay him when they could.

Lester liked to help with the dogs, especially the puppies. He made snug beds for them out of sweet

fresh hay and kept their kennels clean. It was his
job to feed them, after they were weaned from their
mother, the corn pone and buttermilk that were their
favorite foods.

Lester had a hound of his own who had been named
Funny when he was a puppy because of his funny

ways. He was a full-grown foxhound now, and Lester
loved him. He shared his corn pone and buttermilk
with him. Sometimes he shared his pallet on cold
nights when Funny came and crept in with him.

Lester and Big Les had a good time together. They
had been taking care of each other and their dogs
almost as long as Lester could remember, ever since
his mother had died.

Housekeeping was no hard matter. They did most of
their cooking on the open fire. A big pot hung on the

chimney hook, winter and summer, bubbling over a low fire and sending out the smell of something good: rabbit, squirrel, or chicken stew with fat dumplings, or vegetables of several kinds in a rich stirabout.

Yes, Lester and his pappy managed very well, all things considered. When there was no work that had to be done, they went hunting. Big Les kept several fine foxhounds. Lester had just one, but he thought his was the best in the pack, and Big Les didn't dispute it. More than one man had offered to buy Funny, but no amount of cash money would make Lester sell him.

One fine fall day, Lester was sitting on the doorstep braiding a collar for Funny out of groundhog hide.

Big Les had tanned the skin and showed his son how to cut the pieces and weave them together properly. It would be a mighty pretty thing when it was done, Lester thought. He was so busy with his weaving that he didn't see Big Les come up till he spoke to him.

"Son, I want you to go on a little errand for me down to old Mr. Ben Bailey's. Ask him if he's ready to pay for that foxhound I sold him last spring. Tell him I want the money to buy some shoes for you before cold weather. He keeps putting me off every time I see him, but this is a plan that might work. He can see that you are barefooted, and maybe he'll dig the money out of his jeans—if he can stand to part with ten dollars."

"All right," Lester said slowly. He was used to minding his pappy, but this was one job that didn't appeal to him, not at all. He didn't like the notion of calling on old Mr. Ben Bailey and trying to get the much-needed money out of him. He knew all too well the fellow's reputation and hated the very notion of having any words with him.

Lester had heard what the neighbors said about old Mr. Ben Bailey. He had come from Yon-Side about a year ago. At first, everyone had been very friendly with him. They had done him many a good turn, but he never returned a favor. Also, they soon learned it wouldn't do to trust him in a trade.

"He'd cheat a lame man out of his crutch," was a common saying.

No, Lester didn't want to have a thing to do with old Mr. Ben Bailey. "Do I have to mention about needing the money for shoes?" he asked, glancing down at his bare brown feet.

"I think it's the only way to get the ten dollars," said Big Les. "He always has some excuse about not paying when I go to him. He has sold a mule this week, so he's bound to have the money. Now's the very time for you to tackle him."

Lester hung up the unfinished dog collar and took off down the mountain trail with Funny along with him.

When they got to old Ben Bailey's house, smoke was curling from the chimney, so Lester felt quite sure the owner was at home. He went up to the door and knocked, anxious to get the visit over.

In a moment the cabin door opened a small crack, and a foxy face poked out.

"You bringing me a foxhound, Sonny?"

Old Mr. Ben Bailey had tried to buy Funny more than once.

"No-sir-ee!" Lester said. "I've come on other business. Pappy wants the money you owe him for the hound you've already bought. He needs it to buy me a pair of shoes before cold weather!" There—the words were all out in one gulp.

The face in the crack of the door poked itself out a little farther and broke at last into a snaggle-toothed grin. The door opened wider.

"Come in, Sonny. You and your dog, too."

Lester and Funny went in. The fireplace was smoldering with odds and ends of wood. The hearth was unswept. A ragged-looking cat sprawled in the litter of the chimney corner. From somewhere outside came a sound that made Funny's ears prick up.

"I'll tell you about that foxhound your pappy sold me." Old Ben Bailey's voice was loud, as if to cover up the sound that came again. It might have been the low moan of wind around the corner of the cabin, or the whine of a hound dog in distress.

"I'll tell you," the old man said, "that hound dog has got so no-account, he's no good to me at all. I've got him tied up in the yard so that he can't run away till a man from Yon-Side the mountain comes to buy him. I aim to get a little more than your pappy's asking price. I've got to make me a profit on this dog before I let him go. Maybe then I can see my way to paying your pappy. You go back home and tell him that's the best I can do."

Lester turned to go. Funny was pawing at the door, whining to be let out. Once free, he bounded away and around the corner of the house. Lester was close behind him.

There in the middle of the backyard was a pitiful sight to behold: a foxhound tied to a stake in the ground by a rope that gave him little freedom. He must have been there for many days by the look of the wallow in the ground.

Could this dirty, wild-eyed, half-starved looking creature be the same foxhound Big Les had sold last spring? Yes, it was—it must be the same! Funny seemed to know him. He was leaping and barking madly about his friend.

Lester reached down to pat the dog, who pulled on his rope to meet him.

"Be off, be off, you and your dog!" Old Ben Bailey yelled, grabbing a stick. "Be off—be on your way before that hound gets loose!"

His words were no sooner said when the rope snapped in a mad struggle, and the two dogs went dashing away up the mountain trail.

Old Ben Bailey called and called them, but they paid no attention. He tried to whistle them back, but since he had few front teeth, this did no good at all.

"Get my dog back! Get my dog back!" he cried.

In reply, Lester just walked on and out of the yard.

Old Ben Bailey ran after him. "You've got to get my dog and bring him home!" he yelled.

Lester looked over his shoulder. "He's not your dog, and he never was. You never paid for him."

That's all Lester said. It was a very good answer because it was the truth, every word of it.

Old Ben Bailey had no answer to that. He just stood there by his cabin, beating his fists together because he was so mad to think Lester had got the better of him. No one in No-End Hollow had ever done that before. It was quite the surprise for him!

As for Lester, he went along home—the dogs had gotten there before him—and told his pappy all that there was to tell.

How Big Les laughed when he heard it! "I'm proud," he declared. "I'm real proud to have that foxhound back. I'd rather have him back again than have the money from old Ben Bailey. I reckon we can sell a pig and buy you a pair of winter shoes. Nobody would buy this hound till he's fed and fattened awhile."

"Anyway, cold weather's not here yet," laughed Lester. Why, this was only September, and there hadn't even been a light frost.

Nearly all the children of the neighborhood went barefoot during warm weather. Only the older boys and girls wore shoes to school. A boy could run races faster, play games better, and climb a tree quicker if he didn't wear shoes. No use worrying about shoes till the middle of October, when Jack Frost started nipping toes. Just now there was something else to think about.

Lester raced into the house and got all the food he could find in the corner cupboard. There was corn pone and buttermilk and rabbit stew. He put these all into a big bowl and called the dogs to dinner.

Guess which one got the bigger share? I know, and so do you!

You would think that after this experience with old Mr. Ben Bailey that Lester would have been afraid to trust him anymore. The truth is that Big Les, and Lester, too, had no more to do with their neighbor for

many and many a day. They let him strictly alone and
never stopped by to pass the time of day when they
went down the trail by his cabin. If they met him by
happenstance, they said "Howdy" in a mannerly way
and passed on.

"He's a good one to leave alone," Big Les said. "He's
the stingiest man in No-End Hollow. He would skin

a gnat for its hide and tallow. I'll never trade with him again. That's the way to keep from having trouble with such a fellow, leave him alone. Remember what I tell you."

"I will," Lester said. And he meant to mind his pappy, but he didn't know then what was going to happen soon.

The day that Lester was twelve years old, his pappy kept the promise he had been making off and on for two or three years. He let him take off down the trail that leads through No-End Hollow and goes on to Far Beyant, the county seat five miles away. Lester had never been to Far Beyant, but he had heard about it, and he longed to see the strange sights that were there to behold: the houses two or three stories high, the stores with big glass windows, and the rattety-bang trains that went through the town.

"I reckon you can be trusted now to find your way there and back," Big Les told him. "All you do is follow the trail, and don't take any shortcuts or make any talk with strangers. Look around awhile; see all there is to see. Then turn around and come on back."

"I wish you could come along with me, Pappy," said Lester, who had never gone so far from home in his whole life.

"Well, I can't, and you know it," Big Les replied. "Somebody's got to stay and look after Old Min. She's not been feeling well lately, and I've got to stay home and doctor her today." Old Min was expecting puppies that were due to be born almost any day.

"You're not afraid to journey alone, are you?" Big Les turned a keen eye on his son.

"No—no, no sir-ee!" Lester assured him, fearful only that his pappy might change his mind about letting him go on the trip. "I won't be all alone by myself, anyway," he told his pappy, "because I'll have Funny along with me."

"He'll keep you good company," Big Les agreed. Then he slapped his hands together and cried: "Great guns! I had almost forgotten the big birthday surprise I have all ready for you." He went off into the lean-to

kitchen for a minute and came back holding out a
brand-new pair of shoes.

"Got those at Cross Roads Store," he explained
to Lester.

"How did you pay for them?" Lester asked. He
hadn't missed a pig.

"Paid with a promise." Big Les laughed. "Mr. Prater
is mighty anxious to have one of Old Min's pups, and I
promised him one of them."

Lester thanked his pappy for the shoes, put them on
in a hurry, said goodbye, whistled to his dog, and set
off down the trail.

Funny, of course, couldn't understand that this trip
was like no other he and his master had ever taken
before. He thought it was a hunting ramble and ran off
this way and that, trying to pick up a scent. What he
picked up was a locust tree thorn that sent him back
to Lester, whining in a pitiful way and holding up his
right forepaw.

What a happenstance this was! Lester sat down on
a rock and took the trembling Funny into his arms

while he examined the paw. The thorn had gone in so deep that it was hard to get hold of it. Finally, when he pulled it out, poor Funny yelped with pain.

"I wish I had something to put on the sore place," thought Lester, "but we're too far from home to go back there for anything if we're going to Far Beyant today."

Funny only whined in answer, and when Lester put him down, came limping after him.

"What had I better do?" the boy wondered. He couldn't go on with Funny, who had begun to whine again. The dog was in too much pain to travel the trail.

Lester sat down on a stump and took the dog in his lap again. The wounded paw was beginning to bleed.

"Poor Funny." Lester petted him. "You can't go to Far Beyant with me. I guess I'll just have to take you home."

The dog whined mournfully as he licked his sore foot. Then his ears pricked up at a sudden noise. Lester looked up. Old Mr. Ben Bailey came in sight around the bend of the trail.

"Having trouble, Sonny?" he asked in a sympathetic voice as he drew near.

Lester had to explain what had happened.

"Too bad, too bad!" said old Mr. Ben Bailey in a soft, sad tone. "Too bad for you to miss your trip—too bad for the dog to walk at all till his foot is better." His face looked as sad as his voice.

"Listen, Sonny," he said. "It's just a little way, just a hop and jump from my cabin. I'll carry your dog there and doctor up his foot. Got some liniment that I guarantee will help him in a hurry. What do you say?"

What could Lester do? What could he say? He didn't want any favors from old Mr. Ben Bailey. For poor Funny's sake, though, he had to agree.

The dog growled when the man started to pick him up.

"I'll carry him," said Lester, and he did, though the dog was a rather heavy load. He was very glad indeed that it was only a hop and jump to the Bailey cabin. As soon as they got there, the old man brought out a bottle of liniment, dark brown and strong smelling, but Funny wouldn't let him doctor his sore paw. Lester had to put it on, and when he had done this, he used his handkerchief for a bandage.

"Woof!" said the dog then, as if he felt a little better. In a few minutes, he stretched himself out and seemed to go to sleep.

"It's that strong-smelling liniment," explained old Ben Bailey. "He's sniffed enough of it to make him doze a good long while. Listen, Sonny, why don't you leave this dog here with me and go right on to Far Beyant? When you get back from your trip, you'll find him well enough, I'll guarantee, to go on home with you. That liniment heals in a hurry—it's mighty strong stuff."

Lester looked at Funny lying on the floor. He certainly seemed to be having a good nap. Lester hated to leave him, but surely no harm would come to him here. He had little trust in old Mr. Ben Bailey, but this time he seemed to be trying to be kind.

"I'll take good care of your dog, never fear." He smiled at Lester as if he could read his thoughts.

Lester decided to trust him. "I'll be very much obliged," he said, remembering his manners. Then he patted his dog goodbye and took to the trail again.

He got to Far Beyant about high noon and spent an hour or so looking at all the strange town sights. He walked up and down the streets, looking in the

windows of all the stores. He stopped at the yellow depot and waited with a little crowd gathered by the side of the railroad. Soon he heard a whistle and saw the train rushing into sight. What a wonderful sight it was, and what a terrible noise it made! Before he knew what he was doing, Lester clapped his hands over his ears, and everybody laughed. This made Lester feel shy, and he hurried away from the depot as if he had special business he had to see about right then. As he walked off with his hands in his pockets, suddenly his fingers found something that went *jingly-jing!*

Money! Lester hadn't known he had it till this minute. But he guessed right away that his pappy had put it there for him as another birthday surprise! It made Lester happy to find it just now. He took it out and counted it very carefully: five dimes, two nickels, a quarter, and fifteen pennies—a whole dollar. Lester had never felt so rich!

Lester went in. "I want to see that hunting horn you've got in the window," he told the young man who came up to wait on him.

"Yes, sir," the clerk replied. "That's a fine horn, too, I can tell you, although it's not a new one." He picked up the horn and turned it over.

"See what a pretty thing—made from a perfect steer horn, and it has a silver mouthpiece—that alone is worth a dollar."

Lester took it in his hands and looked it over carefully. It was certainly a fine horn as far as looks were concerned. He put it to his lips and blew long and hard.

"Too—oo—toot!"

At the sudden sound, several people who were in the store jumped and looked around. When they saw Lester trying his horn out, they laughed and went on about their business.

Still, Lester couldn't help feeling shy among all these strange people. He didn't like the idea of drawing so much attention to himself.

He turned the hunting horn this way and that. It was certainly a beauty, with its creamy-gold color

and shiny silver mouthpiece. He had never seen a

horn so fine as this, or one that sounded better. How

proud he would be to take this on a hunting trip!

Now he wouldn't have to borrow his pappy's. Then

Lester remembered something. Pappy had lost his

hunting horn on the very last trip they had made. He

had worried a lot about it. Lester had a notion all of

a sudden—a jim-dandy notion. He wanted to think

about it all to himself.

Now he hurriedly paid for the horn, tucked it

securely in an elbow-crook of his arm, and went

on his way.

It was getting late in the afternoon when Lester
came in sight of old Mr. Ben Bailey's cabin again.
When he knocked on the door, it opened a crack.

"Oh, it's you!" said old Mr. Ben Bailey. "Come to get
your dog. Well, young'un, I've got bad news to tell you.
That dog of yours ran away just as soon as he got able.
I tried to holler him back but couldn't do a thing with
him. Reckon he must have gone home."

Lester looked at him hard. Funny wouldn't have done this, he knew. If his dog had got away, he wouldn't have gone back home. No, indeed, he would have tracked his master on the trail to Far Beyant till he caught up with him.

Old Mr. Ben Bailey had done something with Funny. Lester felt certain-sure that he had hidden him, hoping to sell or swap him later on to somebody over the mountain. It wouldn't be the first time such wicked tricks had been suspected of him.

Perhaps the old man guessed that Lester was suspicious, for now he flung wide his cabin door and said with a snaggle-tooth grin:

"Come in, come in, and see for yourself. But you won't find him. Call him—whistle for him!"

The words were a taunt, a dare.

Lester was now so frightened over the fate of his dog that he couldn't utter a word. His throat would have choked had he tried to call. His lips trembled too much to whistle. He looked around, and then with tear-filled eyes, he turned and stumbled out of old Mr.

Ben Bailey's cabin. Suddenly, at the edge of the yard,
Lester stopped. He had an idea. From the elbow-crook
of his arm, he took out the horn.

"Too—oo—oo—toot!" the silvery sweet notes rang
out. They went up and down No-End Hollow and over
the mountainside.

"Too—oo—toot!" Once more Lester blew it—then stopped to listen.

"Boo—oo!" He heard his dog's answer, faint and far away.

Lester started to follow the sound, but old Mr. Ben Bailey didn't realize what he was doing. He watched

the boy lopping off up the trail, then he laughed a big laugh and slammed the door of his cabin.

Lester sounded his hunting horn, again and again, to let his dog know he was coming just as fast as he possibly could. He knew he was on the right trail, for as he went along, Funny's barks became louder and louder. Then he caught sight of the dog. He had been

muzzled and tied to a tree. At the sight of his master,
he leaped and jumped madly. He had gnawed through
the muzzle, but he could not free himself from the
stout chain.

It took Lester several minutes to unfasten him.
While he was doing this, he comforted Funny. "Poor
old fellow! You did your best to get loose, didn't you?
You've had a bad time, and it's partly my fault for
leaving you with old Ben Bailey. But I'll do my best to
make it up to you." He gave Funny a mighty hug, and
the dog licked him and spoke to him with joyful barks
to show that he understood.

The injured paw seemed to be better now, but Lester
carried Funny over the roughest part of the trail as
they hurried home.

At the gate, Lester took his horn and blew it loudly
and clearly. Big Les smiled a welcome as he came to
the door. "Well, I know already what you bought with
your birthday money!"

Big Les took the horn and looked it over admiringly.
"Prettiest hunting horn I've ever seen in all my life,"

he told Lester. "Look at that pure silver mouthpiece! A fine piece of work this is. No telling how old it is. Why, it may have come from England, way back in the days when the early pioneers, our forefathers, came over and settled in these mountains. Yes, sir-ee, son, you've certain-sure got yourself a prize. You can be mighty proud of it."

"*We* can be proud," Lester told him. "I've had a notion about this horn—it's a partnership thing— yours and mine. I want you to have a half share in it because you lost your horn."

Big Les smiled down at his son. "That's what I call a fine notion—a mighty fine notion." Then he raised the hunting horn and blew a blast that could have been heard on the other side of the mountain. It brought all their own dogs on the run.

"They think we're off for a fox hunt right now," Lester laughed.

"Not now, not now," said Big Les, "but we will be before long. Right now I want to go in and finish up cooking supper while you tell all about your trip to Far Beyant."

There was quite a tale to tell. Lester started while
his pappy mixed up a big mess of cornbread. And he
didn't finish till they were sitting down together at the
table while the dogs waited their turn outside the door.

Big Les listened and shook his head. "That
scoundrel, old Ben Bailey! That kind of man needs to
learn his lesson on how to deal with honest folk."

When the folks in No-End Hollow heard about old
Ben Bailey's latest and meanest trick, it made them
sure-enough mad. They said he ought to be punished,
for stealing as often as he did.

Maybe old Ben Bailey heard what folks were saying
about him, too—for he left in a hip-and-hurry, all by
himself, and he didn't tell a soul where he went!

The Right House for Rowdy

By May Justus

First published in 1960

© 2018 Jenny Phillips

www.thegoodandthebeautiful.com

Illustrations by Jean Tamburine

For all the boys and girls
who have asked me to write
another dog story.

Tib Turner lived with his folks in a little log cabin halfway up No-End Hollow. To some people it would have seemed a very small house. It had only two rooms with an open porch, or dogtrot, between them. It was big enough for the Turners: Father, who was tall; Mother, who was short; and Tib, who was nearly ten and about the proper size for his age, as everybody said.

Yes, the little log house was roomy enough for the Turners' way of living. Rowdy, Tib's hound pup, had the dogtrot, a very fine place for him to take naps on summer days or watch out for the chickens when they tried to slip outside the paling fence which ran around the house.

Mr. Turner praised Rowdy for protecting the garden, and Mrs. Turner liked him for guarding her flower beds.

But this is not a summertime tale. No, indeed. It starts out on a very frosty morning of a late November day.

The Turners were just sitting down to a hearty breakfast and paying full attention to it because it was extra good—hoecakes made from new cornmeal, fresh butter, and molasses. A roaring fire burned in the kitchen room to drive out the early morning chill.

"Boo-oo," Rowdy whined through a crack in the door that opened into the dogtrot.

Tib looked across the table with a plea on his face. He looked at his mother first.

Mrs. Turner smiled. "All right, we'll forget rules this morning," she said. "Let him in to warm by the fire."

"But no feeding under the table," Father warned Tib with a stern look, "or out he goes again."

"No, sir-ee!" Tib promised before he dashed to let his hound pup in. He knew he and Rowdy had better

behave, or they would get into trouble double-quick!
But knowing, too, that his dog would be hungry as
well as chilly, Tib took a hoecake from his plate to toss
him before letting him inside.

"Yip-yap!" Rowdy capered into the cozy kitchen
and danced and pranced with joyful wiggles all over
the hearth.

Tib went back to his breakfast but kept looking over
his shoulder at Rowdy, who still shook and shivered as
if he would never thaw out.

"I guess he nearly froze to death last night out there
in the dogtrot," Tib said with a choke in his throat. His
dog was not a year old yet, and this would be his first
taste of winter.

"Maybe we could let him sleep inside tonight," he
said with a pleading look at his father.

Mr. Turner shook his head. "It would only spoil him
to let him get in the habit of sleeping inside the house.
A good watchdog needs to be outside on the lookout
for danger. Since we've had Rowdy, no wild varmints
have been in the chicken roost."

"He's a fine watchdog, certain-sure," agreed Mrs. Turner, "and we ought to take good care of him."

Tib gave his mother a grateful look.

"Lady and Gravy have a stable, and the chickens have a shed," said Mother. "Seems like Rowdy ought to have a house of his own."

Lady was Mother's pet cow. Gravy, the mule, belonged to Father. Lady had been named for her gentle nature, Gravy for his coloring, which was just the shade of brown ham gravy.

Mrs. Turner smiled at Tib. "I guess that would suit Rowdy. You and your father can talk about it while I clear the dishes away."

"It's high time the dog had a house," Father said. "We ought to build it before cold weather. By the feel of the air, Old Man Winter is already on his way."

"Let's do it today," Tib said eagerly. "Let's do it this morning."

This would be a fine time for the job, since it was the week of fall vacation, when school closed so the children could help get the late crops in before winter.

Father munched the last bite of his hoecake and pushed back his plate.

"We can't do it right away. First, we've got to cut down a sapling or two and chop up logs to make the doghouse. And before we can do any chopping at all, we've got to sharpen the ax. It's so dull, it wouldn't cut a cornstalk."

Tib understood. This meant a spell at the grindstone with Father holding the ax against the stone to sharpen the blade while he, Tib, turned the handle. It was a job he had little liking for, but this was no time to complain.

"Yes, sir-ee!" he agreed.

To sharpen a dull ax takes quite a while, especially on a cold morning. At first Tib whistled a tune as he turned the grindstone against the edge of the ax. But soon he didn't feel like whistling at all. The cold bit the tips of his fingers, and he began to turn the grindstone more and more slowly.

Finally, Mr. Turner said, "Let's stop and rest ourselves for a minute." He blew on his hands to warm

them, and Tib did the same. This took the sting out of the cold and made their fingers limber so they could work better.

And then, right in the middle of their job, came Uncle Josh Evans, making his way down the mountain trail.

"Here comes somebody who is likely to stop and entertain us awhile," said Mr. Turner.

Uncle Josh was no real kin to the Turners, but everyone called him Uncle out of respect for his age. He claimed to be over ninety years old, but he was spry as a squirrel, and was noted as a great talker and a teller of tall tales.

Tib was glad Uncle Josh had happened by. He hoped he would get to talking and tell about some of the wonderful things that had happened to him.

Perhaps Uncle Josh guessed the boy's thoughts, for after a mannerly greeting, he sat down on a nearby stump and looked thoughtfully at Tib. All of a sudden, he jumped up.

"Sonny, let me do that job just to show you how well an old codger can do it!" he cried.

While Uncle Josh turned the grindstone, Tib explained all about the plan to cut logs for the doghouse.

Uncle Josh listened and cast a sharp eye in the boy's direction. "I made me a doghouse once upon a time from a hoe handle," he said.

"A hoe handle!" Tib cried. Mr. Turner smiled.

"A snake-bit hoe handle this was," Uncle Josh said. "Well, I might as well tell you the whole tale. This was the way it happened. I killed a copperhead one day while I was hoeing my corn patch. Right after that, I noticed the handle of my hoe was getting bigger and bigger. You know why? I guessed right away— the poison from the bite of that copperhead. Well, the handle got so big that I couldn't hold it. It got so big that it busted the shank, and the head o' the hoe fell off. I threw that old handle away and went and made me another one. Thought no more about it for a week or so. Then, by happenstance, I was walking by the fence one day and saw the snake-bit hoe

handle a-lying where I had thrown it. At first I didn't
recognize it. Why not? Because it had swelled and
swelled and swelled with all that copperhead poison
in it, till by this time, that hoe handle was as big as a
log—a mighty big log, I can tell you! Well, I hauled it
off to the lumber mill—took two stout mules to pull
it—and had it properly sawed into a stack of lumber.
Had enough to build me a corn crib."

"I thought you made a doghouse!" Tib cried.

Uncle Josh nodded. "That's the way it turned out.
You see, I painted the corn crib. The turpentine in the
paint took nearly all the swelling out of the wood. The
lumber shrank and shrank. Before the day was over,
my corn crib was just the right size for Scooter, my
foxhound pup. All I had to do was nail on some slats
to close up the sides, make a peaked roof, and put in
the right size door."

"You and your tall tales!" Mr. Turner scoffed, but he
couldn't help laughing with Tib.

"That was a fine, funny tale, Uncle Josh," Tib said.
"I like tall tales—the taller, the better. I bet that was a
mighty fine doghouse."

Uncle Josh nodded, and his blue eyes twinkled under his shaggy gray brows. "As I remember," he said, "it suited Scooter all right."

Mr. Turner tested the ax blade carefully between a thumb and finger. "Sharp enough now," he said, "to do a real good job."

Uncle Josh pulled a hair from his head and snapped it over the ax blade.

"Yep!" he nodded. "It'll cut like a hot knife in a hunk o' butter. I wish," he added, "that I had an ax half as good as this one."

"Well, if you have a dull ax, bring it over and sharpen it on our grindstone. I'll turn the wheel," offered Tib.

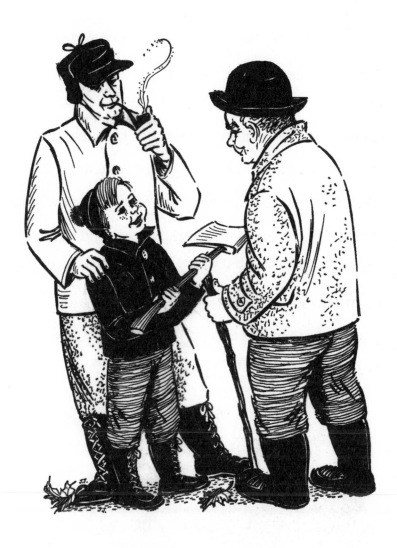

"Yes," Mr. Turner said, "you do that, Uncle Josh. One good turn deserves another."

"Many thanks," Uncle Josh replied. "But I've got no ax—at least only a broken one—and what's worse, a broken ridgepole in the roof of my cabin. I may as well tell you," he went on, "I came here to borrow your ax to cut a tree for a new ridgepole. That roof is likely to crash down on my head any day unless I get it mended."

Uncle Josh stopped short as if he were out of breath.

Tib and his father looked at each other and nodded.

"We'd be glad to lend you our ax to fix that roof," said Mr. Turner. "Rowdy's house can wait."

The old man smiled warmly. As he started up the trail, he called back over his shoulder, "I'll do my best to finish that job today and return your ax tomorrow."

Tib and his father smiled back, waving as Uncle Josh disappeared from view.

That afternoon an icy wind blew down No-End Hollow. By night the air was freezing cold. Tib was worried. Rowdy couldn't stay out in the dogtrot tonight. His folks wouldn't want him in the cabin either. Then Tib got a notion: Maybe the dog would like a bed of hay down at the barn.

Mr. Turner said it was a good idea, if Rowdy behaved himself and didn't try to bother the mule.

Mrs. Turner was somewhat more concerned about Lady. She had an excitable nature, although she was a gentle cow.

Tib knew his parents were remembering Rowdy's tricks as a puppy, but Tib wasn't worried about his behavior now that he was nearly grown. It had been a long time since he had chased the animals, nipped the mule's heels, or tried swinging himself from the tip of Lady's tail.

So it was decided at last that Rowdy should have a bed in the corner of the barn stall. The stall was big and roomy, with a low partition down the middle so that the animals should not get in each other's way.

Rowdy seemed happy enough in his sleeping quarters, all snuggled down in a big bed of hay with an old quilt to cover him.

"Good night, old fellow." Tib gave him a hug and farewell pat before he hurried away to his own cozy bed. It made him glad to know that Rowdy had a corner in the barn, even if he didn't yet have a house of his own.

Just what happened at the barn that night nobody ever knew for certain, although Rowdy was blamed for the trouble that came about.

Tib's father brought the bad news back to the house next morning when he rushed into the kitchen swinging an empty milk pail.

"The cow's gone—the mule, too! They've broken the barn door open, and there's not a hide nor hair of either one in sight!"

"Oh! What happened? What caused the trouble?" Mrs. Turner cried.

As if to answer her, Rowdy bolted into the kitchen.

"That pesky pup—he's to blame, I reckon!" Mr. Turner grumbled. "He must have scared the animals into a fit, to make them break out and run away."

"Yes, yes, that must have been the way the trouble started," she agreed. "That pup has been up to his old-time tricks. Get out, you mischief-maker!" she cried, starting to chase Rowdy from the room.

At the door the dog ran into Tib, who had been standing by, too troubled to say a word. Now he grabbed his pup and ran from the kitchen into the dogtrot.

"The safest place for us both," he said, "is outside."

"Woof!" barked Rowdy with a happy shiver, glad to find himself in his master's arms.

Tib felt sure that Rowdy hadn't meant any mischief, even if he had made the animals break out of the barn.

"It was mostly my fault," Tib thought to himself. "It wasn't a good idea to let him sleep with Lady and Gravy at the barn."

All of a sudden, the dog in his arms began to wiggle so hard that Tib set him down on the dogtrot floor.

"Woof!" he barked. His nose began to quiver, and his ears pricked up.

Tib knew these signals well. Rowdy had caught the scent or sound of something down in the hollow.

The next moment, he was off with a bark, and Tib followed with a yell.

When Tib and his dog came back up the hollow a little later, they weren't by themselves. First came Lady, then Gravy, next Rowdy, who had rounded them up (at a safe distance from their heels), and finally Tib, who had a hard time trying to keep up. It didn't take them long to reach home.

Mr. Turner ran from the barn. Mrs. Turner ran from the cabin.

"Lady is all right. Gravy is, too," Tib said, all in one breath, just to save his parents the trouble of asking questions.

But his father asked one anyway. "Aren't you cold and tired?"

And his mother: "Aren't you awfully hungry?"

"Yes," Tib replied. "Rowdy is, too."

Father laughed. "You both go ahead and have a good warm-up and a late breakfast. Your mother and I will see to the animals."

Tib knew that his mischievous pup was now forgiven. But Rowdy couldn't sleep at the barn anymore. That plan hadn't worked out to the satisfaction of anyone.

"Maybe we can build the doghouse today," Tib thought hopefully as he went into the warm kitchen with Rowdy at his heels, sniffing the good smells.

Tib found a batch of hoecakes, all brown and crunchy, several pieces of crispy bacon, and a pot of sassafras tea still warm on the back of the stove. He divided with Rowdy, who gobbled the bread and meat but refused the sassafras tea. He let his dog eat before the fire because he was still a-tremble with cold.

When they were both fed and warm, Tib dashed out with the dog at his heels and met his parents coming from the barn.

"Let's build Rowdy's house today!" he said to his father.

Mr. Turner nodded. "We'll get to work," he said, "just as soon as Uncle Josh returns the ax."

"Whoop—ee—hurrah!" Tib shouted. "Do you hear that, Rowdy? You're going to have a house! A house of your very own. What do you think about that?"

"Yip-yap!" Rowdy yelped, going around in circles as if he fully understood each word his master said.

The sun rose over the mountain peak. Tib and Rowdy found a warm seat on the back doorstep and watched the winding trail that led toward Uncle Josh Evans' house. Time went by—a long, long time. The sun rose higher and higher. But there was no sight of Uncle Josh coming down the Hollow Trail.

Finally Tib's father said, "There's no use waiting any longer on Uncle Josh and wasting a lot of time. There's a patch of corn that's ready to be gathered. We'll work there till Uncle Josh comes."

Tib followed his father to the corn patch. They started picking the ripe ears into sacks. A little later on, these would be stored in the corn crib and used for bread all winter, as well as to feed the stock.

Tib liked this work all right. He liked to help his father, but he wished they were busy right now doing another job. He couldn't help watching for Uncle Josh with the ax over his shoulder. But the whole morning passed, and still there was no sight of him.

"What could have happened, do you think?" Tib asked his father.

"Reckon that new ridgepole took a lot more time than Uncle Josh thought it would," Mr. Turner answered. "We've just got to be patient. A man who lives to be ninety isn't quite so spry as a nine-year-old boy, you know."

Tib tried to be patient as he went on working in the corn patch. But he couldn't keep his eyes off the trail. Still no sign of Uncle Josh.

At last it was time for dinner—a very good one. Mother had made a pot of stirabout: bacon and corn

and beans, seasoned with herbs. A tasty dish. Father had three helpings, but Tib didn't feel as hungry as he usually did.

"Could we make the doghouse in half a day?" Tib asked his father, which showed that his thoughts were not on his food.

"Oh, I think so," his father replied. "It won't be too big a job after we get the logs cut."

If only Uncle Josh would hurry and bring their ax home!

Tib and his father went back to finish their work in the corn patch. When the corn was all gathered, they hauled it to the barn and stored it in the corn crib. By this time the day was nearly over. The sun ball was going down behind Big Twin. A cold wind blew up No-End Hollow and stung their hands and faces as Tib and his father started home.

"By the feel of that wind, we're going to have a colder night than last," said Mr. Turner.

"Where's Rowdy going to sleep?" Tib asked him. This was the question that had been troubling him more and more as night was drawing on.

He couldn't be put in the barn again. There was the chicken shed—but it wouldn't do to try that. If the pup were to start chasing chickens, there would be fuss and feathers all over the place.

"Let's look around," said his father, "and see if we can't find some place where we can tuck him in."

Tib's eyes fell upon something in a corner of the yard.

"There's that old empty beehive," he said. "If we turned it over, Rowdy could crawl inside—and he would be warm and snug."

"The very thing!" Mr. Turner agreed. Like most beehives in the mountains, this one had been sawed from a big hollow log. It was easy to roll the log against the house in a warm chimney corner outside. When it was all ready, Tib called his dog.

"This is your sleeping place tonight," he told Rowdy, who crawled inside and settled himself as if he understood.

Tib awoke in the middle of the night and heard the wind huffing and puffing around the corners of the cabin. It rattled the boards of the roof and whistled through the cracks. Tib snuggled deeper into his feather bed. He felt cozy and snug, and hoped Rowdy was, too.

Bright and early next morning, Tib ran out to the chimney corner to see about his dog.

But Rowdy wasn't there—and neither was the beehive. Tib rubbed his eyes and looked around the yard. There was no sign of his dog anywhere about.

Tib gave a yell that brought his parents running. His mother was tying an apron on. His father was wearing one shoe.

"What—?"

"What—?" they both cried. But before they could finish their questions, Tib showed them the empty chimney corner.

"Look! Rowdy's gone!" He couldn't keep from crying.

"Oh!" cried his mother. "The dog's gone, certain-sure. Some thief must have stolen him."

"And my beehive, too," said his father. "Right after

breakfast we'll go and search the whole neighborhood. Somebody might be able to help us."

Mr. and Mrs. Turner went back into the cabin, but Tib lingered in the chimney corner for a minute.

All of a sudden, his ears caught a sound above the whistle of the wind. It sounded in the direction of the jump-off, a steep rocky place beyond the backyard which sloped into No-End Hollow.

Tib ran to the jump-off and leaned over a ledge of rocks to look down. Then he saw it—the beehive had lodged between two trees on its runaway trip.

Tib scrambled down the sides of the jump-off and tore down the hollow in a hurry, till it's a thousand wonders that he didn't happen to break both legs.

"Boo-oo-oo!" Rowdy's bark of distress grew louder and louder.

"I'm coming—I'm coming!" Tib called.

It took less than a minute to dislodge the beehive and free the dog, who seemed no worse for his rolling ride down the hollow, to judge from his capers. He

returned his master's hugs with joyful wags and
wiggles and whines which Tib understood.

They left the beehive behind and scrambled out
of the hollow, up the side of the jump-off, and into
the backyard. Then Tib and Rowdy dashed into the
kitchen. Mrs. Turner dropped a hoecake.

"Praise Him above!" she cried. "The dog is found, and the boy is back!"

Rowdy grabbed the hoecake and gobbled it up, but Mrs. Turner never even hinted that the proper place for dogs to eat was outside.

"He's a lucky dog," Mr. Turner said, "that none of his bones were broken. I bet he's the only dog that ever had such a ride."

"How did it happen, do you suppose? Was it the wind," asked Tib, "that rolled the beehive right out of our back yard?"

Mr. Turner chuckled. "I've got a pretty good notion that Rowdy squirmed about till he started the log rolling. And the wind may have helped it on its way."

"I'm sorry about the beehive—I'm afraid it's cracked," said Tib.

"Never mind," said his father. "We haven't any bees that need a new home right now. And I don't think Rowdy will ever want to sleep in a hollow log again."

Rowdy settled himself in a corner of the hearthstone while Tib finished breakfast.

"I do wish," the boy said, "that we could build that doghouse today. I wish that Uncle Josh Evans would finish his job in a hip-and-hurry, and bring our ax back home."

"He's had it long enough, I think," said Mr. Turner, "but I wouldn't want him to bring it back before he finished his job."

"I could go and see how he is getting along," said Tib. "Maybe I could help him to get his work done. Then I could bring the ax home and save him the trouble."

"That's a good idea," his father said. "Go along and lend the old fellow a helping hand."

"I could get there and back a lot faster if I rode Gravy," Tib said.

"Well, I don't need the mule today. You may ride him," his father agreed.

"Whoopee!" shouted Tib. With Rowdy he dashed out the door and headed for the barn.

A few minutes later he rode down the trail of No-End Hollow toward Uncle Josh Evans' cabin. Rowdy raced ahead. By and by they came in sight of the little clearing where the old man's cabin stood.

"The roof looks all right," Tib thought. "I guess he got it mended."

But what was going on back of the house in the other side of the yard? It didn't sound like an ax—no, it must be a hammer. Then Uncle Josh came around the corner of the house.

"Come in—come in!" he called, "you and your dog. I've got something here to show you. Tie your mule so he can't get loose, and come on into the yard."

He led the way around the house, and Tib followed.
Then Tib stopped still, and his eyes nearly popped out
of his head.

"Look-a-there! Did you ever see a finer doghouse?"
Uncle Josh asked him. "It's Scooter's old house, but I
had to split some new boards for a roof. That's why I
kept the ax so long. I wanted to save you the trouble of
building a new house for your dog, especially when,

as I could tell, you liked the notion of this one I made
from the hoe handle I was telling about the other day."

"You mean this is for him—for Rowdy?" Tib cried.

"Yep!" Uncle Josh replied. "I've saved this house a
long time—ever since Scooter died. Now that it's got
a new roof, it's just as good as ever. It's a thank-gift
to you for helping me get my own house fixed up
for winter."

Tib looked at the doghouse with shining eyes. Then
he looked at Uncle Josh Evans.

"This is a mighty fine doghouse, Uncle Josh. I bet
Rowdy is the only dog with a house made from a

snake-bit hoe handle! I'm mighty much obliged to you," he added, not forgetting his manners.

Just then Rowdy, who had slipped inside the doghouse, poked his head out the door. "Woof!" He gave a joyful bark.

"I reckon Rowdy wants to thank you for his house, Uncle Josh," Tib said. "He's found the right house for Rowdy at last."

More Books from The Good and the Beautiful

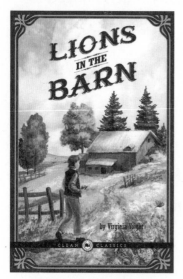

Lions in the Barn
by Virginia Voight

The Great Death-Defying Signor Joseph Dobbinelli Most Daring Animal Trainer in the World,
the sign reads, and Sr. Dobbinelli is in need of a good, stout winter barn for his circus animals. Clay and his family have just the barn in Connecticut, but do they have what it takes to care for lions and tigers?

In this delightful tale of adventure and family life on the farm, Clay is in for some lessons on responsibility and wild animal training.

Ernie Brett never could have guessed what surprises lay in store for his family when his father moves them from the shanty mining camp of Skillet Gulch over the hills to Nugget to settle on a new ranch. Set in the high Rocky Mountains of Colorado Territory during the gold rush years, this novel explores some of the risks, hardships, joys, and pastimes of the era. Through hard work and ingenuity, Ernie and Papa are able to provide for the family and improve the farm. When tragedy strikes, will the Bretts have the courage to stay on their beloved ranch?

Over the Hills to Nugget
by Aileen Fisher